To Zat and Nellie
for playing along

This book is set in Century 725/Monotype; Grilled Cheese BTN/Fontbros; Typography of
Coop, Fink, Neutraface/House Industries

Printed in Malaysia
Reinforced binding

First Edition, June 2010
20 19 18 17 16 15
FAC-029191-20055 | ISBN: 978-1-4231-1991-3

Library of Congress Cataloging-in-Publication Data on file.

Visit www.hyperionbooksforchildren.com and www.pigeonpresents.com

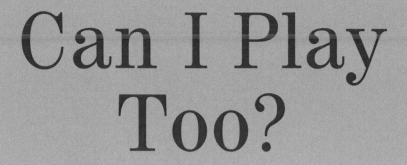

Can I Play Too?

By **Mo Willems**

An **ELEPHANT & PIGGIE** Book

Hyperion Books for Children / *New York*
AN IMPRINT OF DISNEY BOOK GROUP

3

4

I love playing catch with friends!

I will throw.

Can I play too?

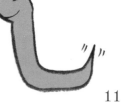

12

13

But . . .

We are
playing
catch.

17

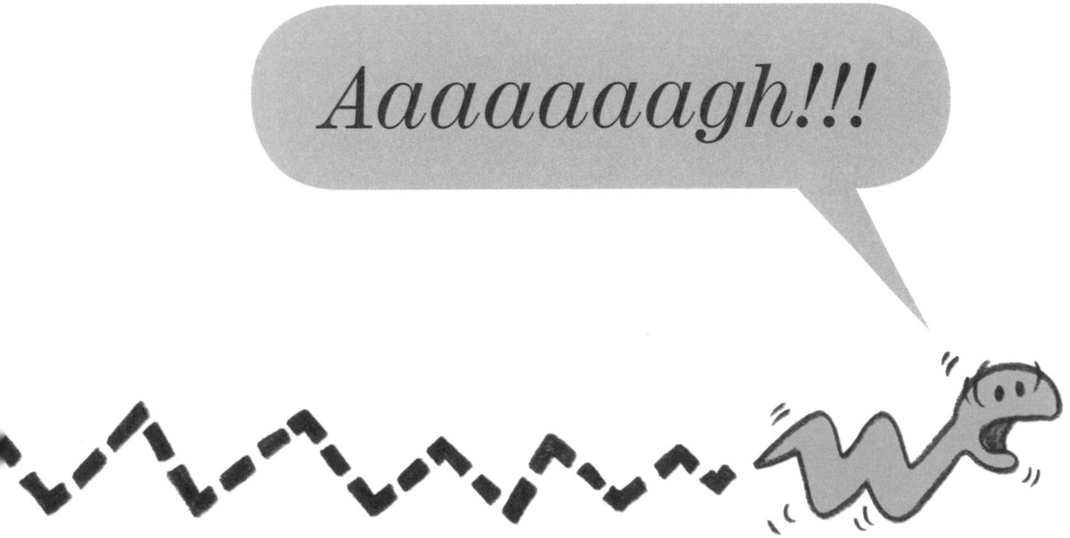
Aaaaaaagh!!!

22

But I
can *try.*

27

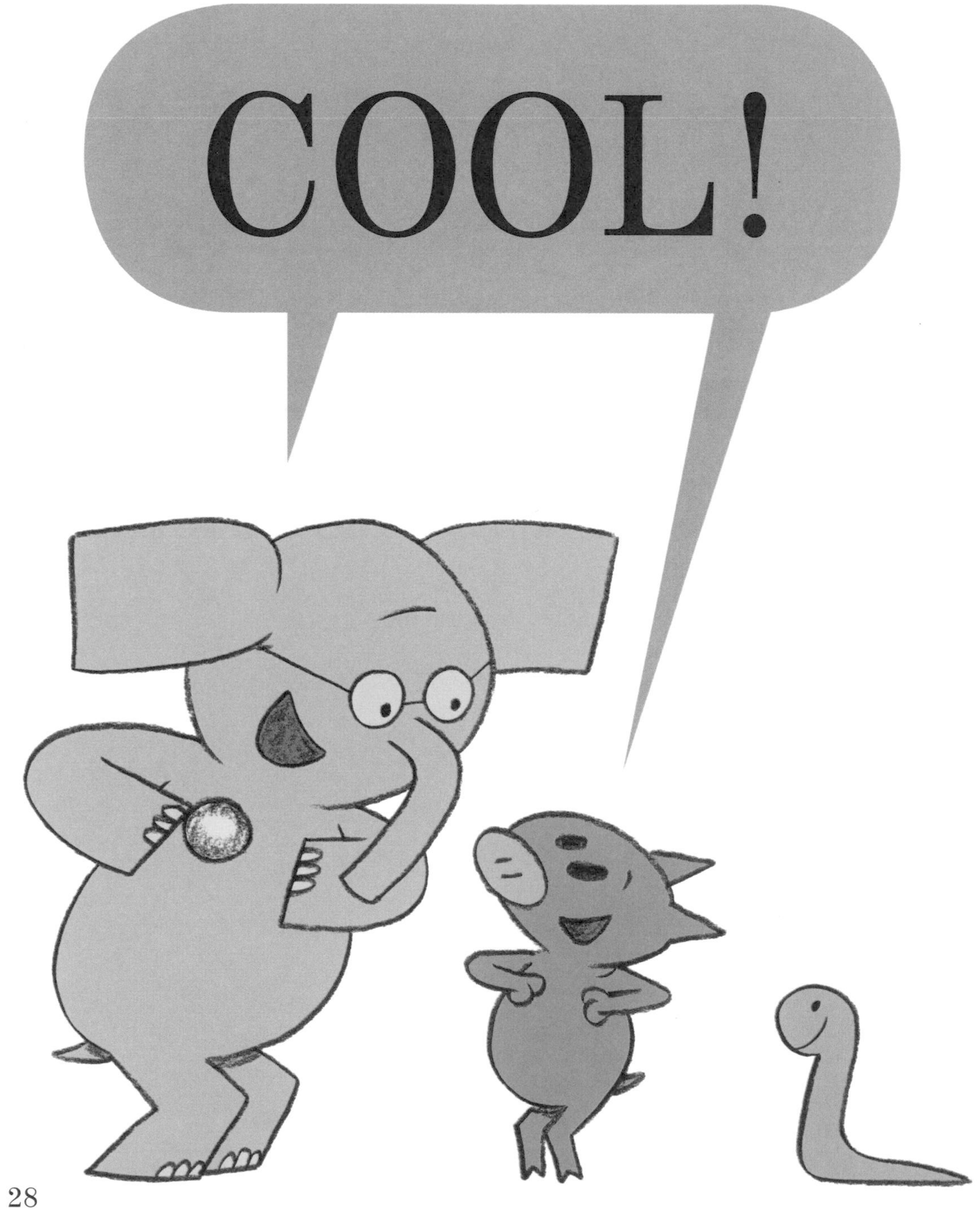
COOL!

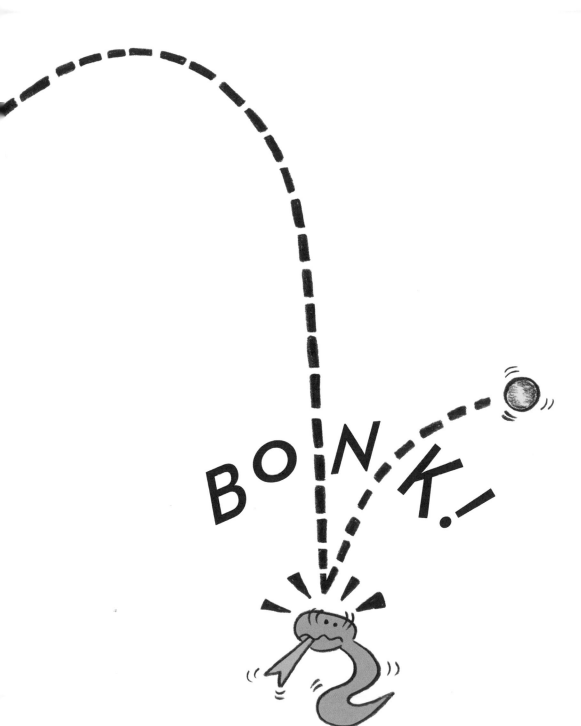

BONK!

33

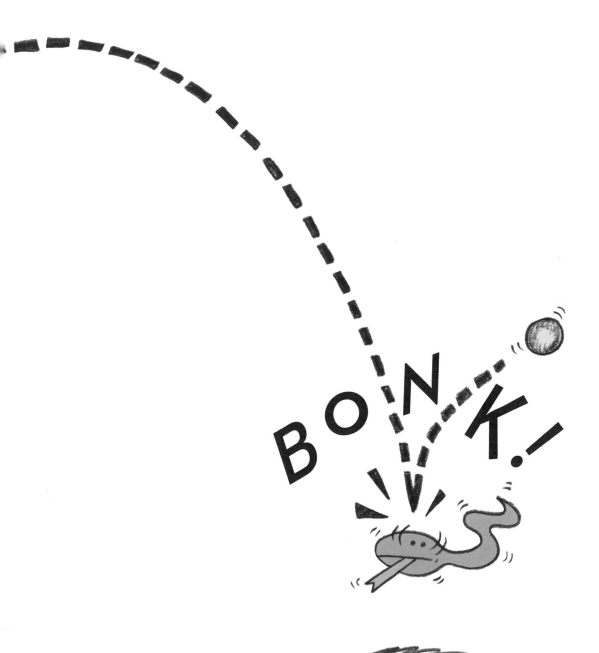

BONK!

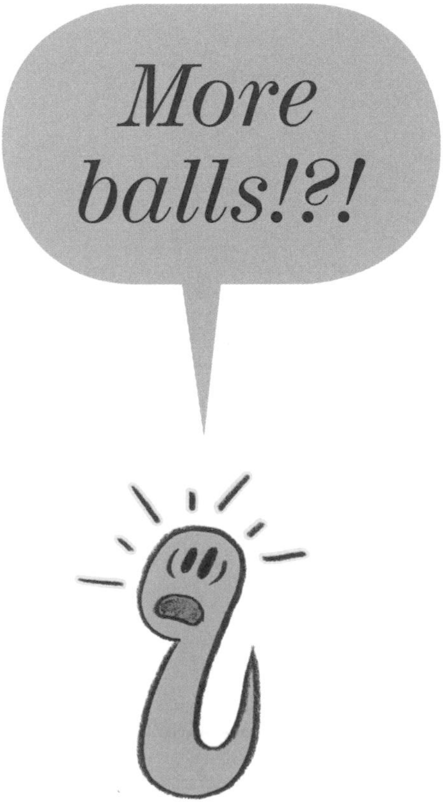
More balls!?!

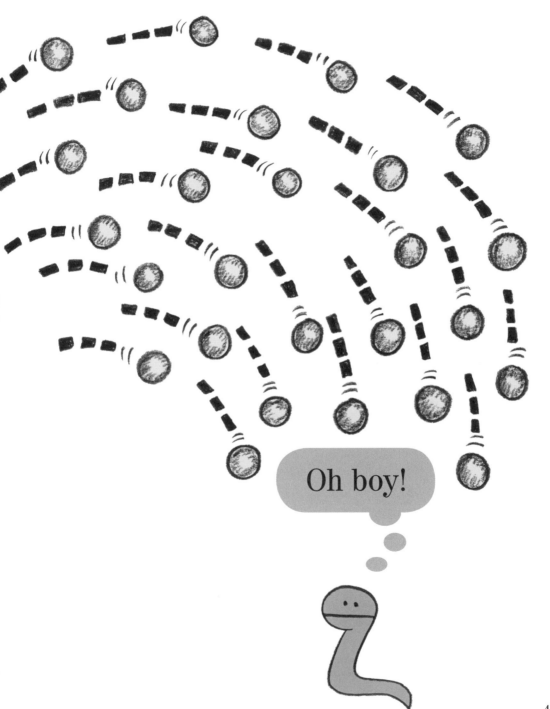

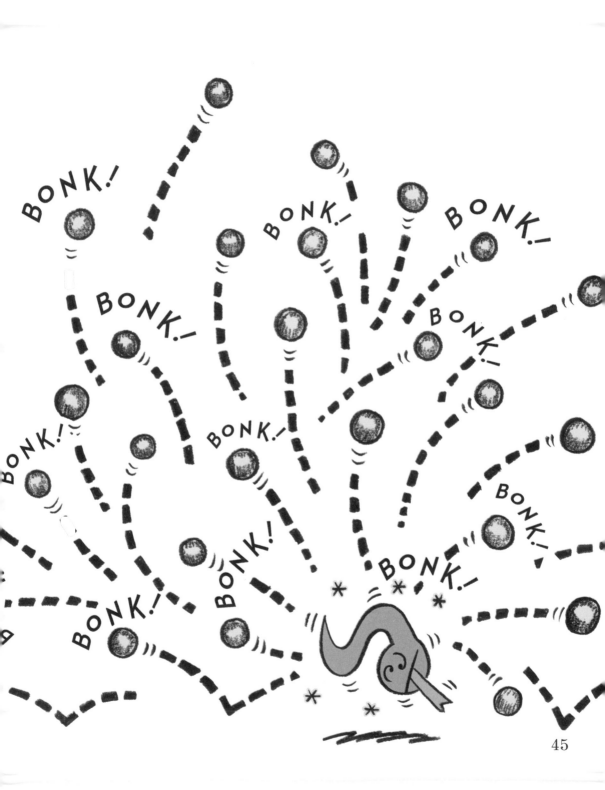

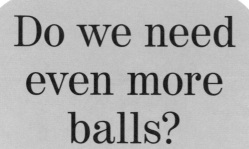

50

51

52

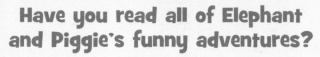

Have you read all of Elephant and Piggie's funny adventures?